Why Butterflies go by on Silent Wings

by Marguerite W. Davol

illustrated by Rob Roth

SCHOLASTIC INC.

New York Toronto London Auckland Sydney
Mexico City New Delhi Hong Kong Buenos Aires

ISBN 0-439-56073-X

Text copyright © 2001 by Marguerite W. Davol.
Illustrations copyright © 2001 by Robert Roth. All rights reserved.
Published by Scholastic Inc. SCHOLASTIC and associated logos
are trademarks and/or registered trademarks of Scholastic Inc.

12 11 10 9 8 7 6 5 4 3 2   4 5 6 7 8 9/0

Printed in the U.S.A.   10

First Scholastic printing, March 2004

Book design by Mina Greenstein. The text of this book is set in 16 point Weiss.
The illustrations were painted in watercolor and then designed
and composed digitally in Photoshop.

For Bob—and for all who revel in the sunset
or a bright blue sky.
For all who pause to marvel
as a butterfly glides by.

                —M.W.D.

This book is for my parents,
Ronald and Betty Roth—
To my father, who is "Larger than Life,"
and to my mother, "Sweet as Honey."

                —R.R.

Back when the world was young, it was noisy. Very noisy. Forests and fields everywhere throbbed with the loud sounds of animals—hoots and roars, screeches and yowls. But the noisiest place of all was the country that lay between the Mountains of the Mist and the Singular Sea. There, all day long, the air was thick with a deafening buzz and whirr of bees and the whine of flies.

Overhead, howling monkeys leaped from tree to tree. "Hi-yi! Look at us climb," they bragged, so loudly that the leaves shook. "We're above all you other animals."

Far below, the hyenas, not to be out-shouted, hooted with laughter. "Who cares?" they jeered. "Pray, which of you dares climb down—to eat with us?"

Lions roared a warning. "R-r-rather you'll be eaten. R-r-rather you monkeys'll be hyenas' prey. Or our-r-rs."

Ambling past, the elephants trumpeted ceaselessly, "Out of our way! Out of our way!"

And over all the noise, each animal louder than the other, the thundering hooves of the wildebeests made the earth shake. What a din! In fact, the country between the Mountains of the Mist and the Singular Sea was so noisy that all the animals' ears twitched and thrummed with the incessant sounds. From anteater to zebra, each creature searched for ways to shut out the noise, but none succeeded—except for the elephants, who rolled up their huge ears like window shades.

But of all the noisy creatures in the land, the butterflies made the loudest, most annoying sounds. Day after day, as the tedious drab butterflies flew from flower to flower, they boasted and argued among themselves—loudly.

One rain-washed morning, a butterfly whisked its wings and screeched, "Look at me fly! I'm the fastest!"

"Hoo—who says so!" another said. "I can beat you with one wing tied behind me!"

"Well, I gather more nectar than any of you," one plump butterfly said loudly and plunged its long drinking tube deep into the heart of a flower.

From its perch on an overripe banana, another shrilled, "You don't either. I do!"

And the smallest butterfly of all, its voice more a squeak than a shriek, said, "Me too!"

Pausing beside a puddle on a steamy afternoon, a wide-winged butterfly boasted, "Look! I'm the most magnificent of all." Whereupon a battalion of butterflies shoved that one aside. Pushing and preening, admiring their reflections in the water, they shrieked, "No, me!" "Let me see!" "I'm the most magnificent butterfly in the country."

As day followed day, the noisy creatures continued to swoop from flower to flower, their shrill sounds clouding the air. However, every few hours or so, all the butterflies gathered to rest. They clustered, hundreds of them, in a Bingalou tree that towered over the plains. Hanging from the broad-limbed tree like dull brown fluttering leaves, were the butterflies finally quiet? Of course not! They were still boasting, still arguing— oh, how they argued!

"It's hot!"

"No, it's not. It's chilly."

"Don't be silly—it's hot!"

What a din! Their sounds were more raucous than those of a flock of crows or a gaggle of angry geese. Worse, they even argued about which of them was the loudest.

"My voice is so loud, it smashes bananas."

"Well, my voice can split coconuts."

"Mine is even louder—it makes army ants march the other way."

"But I'm the loudest in the land!"

And as always, the smallest butterfly squeaked, "Me too!"

From sunup to sundown and far into the night, hundreds of shrill butterfly voices filled the air, drowning out all the other whistles, howls and growls, caws and coos. Not one butterfly ever stopped screeching long enough to look up at the monkeys swinging through the treetops or down at the herds of wildebeests. Not one butterfly ever paused long enough to enjoy the pink and orange of a sunset or the bright blue of the sky.

Now, from time to time, two small figures crossed the noisy country between the Mountains of the Mist and the Singular Sea on the way to visit old Juju, their grandmum. Hand in hand, the sister and little brother hurried along, wincing at the ear-splitting sounds all around them. The boy would whimper, "Noisy. Too noisy!"

By chance one day, the little boy brushed against the butterflies clinging to the Bingalou tree. Oh, my! Within seconds the angry butterflies crowded around the children. Flapping against their faces and covering their arms, the creatures screeched, "Out of our way. Go away!"

Frantic, the girl brushed off the thick cloud of fluttering creatures, muttering, "Leave us alone, you ugly, noisy things!" Then, their hands pressed tight against each ear to shut out those voices that out-howled the monkeys and out-yowled the hyenas, the children ran. Fast!

ONE DAY dark storm clouds gathered, piling high in the west. The wind began to howl, louder than any animal in the land. Driving the rain before it, the wind flattened the grasses and shook the trees. Lightning sliced the sky, and thunder *br-oomed*, making the earth tremble.

Nearly blown from their perch in the Bingalou tree, the frightened butterflies clung together, struggling against the tremendous storm. They waited in silent terror for the storm to pass. Finally the wail of the wind began to lessen, but just as the last sheets of rain headed east, lightning struck! *ZINGG–CRACK!*

That Bingalou split right down the middle and fell with an enormous *CRASH–WHANG!* All the butterflies, flung from the toppled tree, fell to the ground.

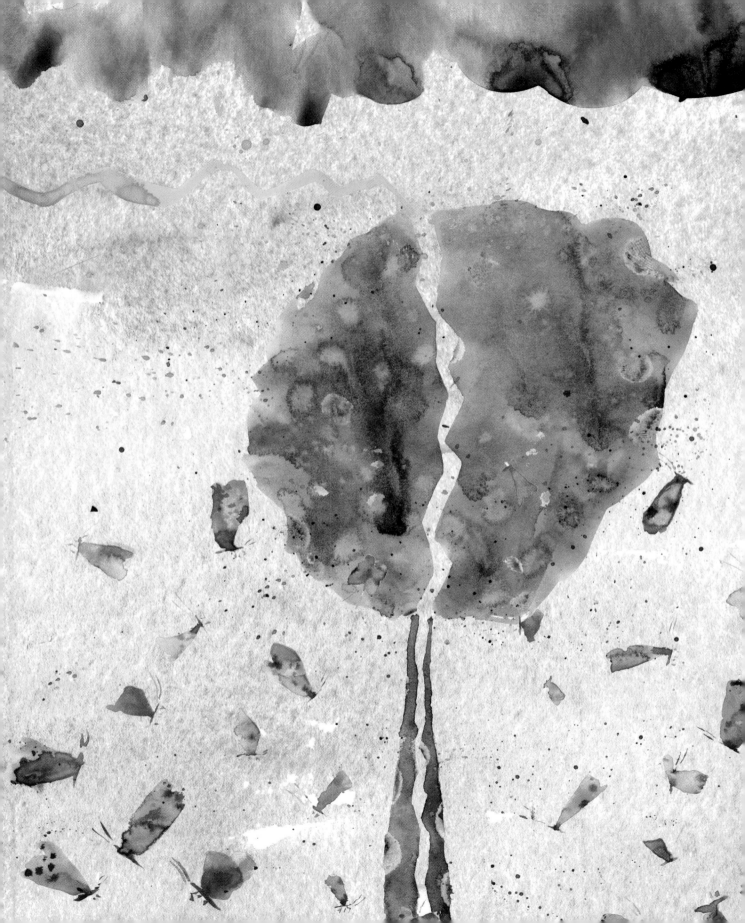

For several moments nothing stirred,
as the huge sound of the crash echoed and
reechoed across the plains. No other sound was
heard except for one final faint rumble of thunder in
the distance. Every creature in the land had been
stunned into silence!

Wet and bedraggled, the butterflies slowly crawled

out of the mud where they'd been tossed. Some climbed onto an overhanging rock. Others inched up the stalks of bright flowers or tall grasses or struggled to nearby trees. They spread their wings to dry.

In silence the butterflies watched the sun edge from behind the clouds, gold against the blue sky. In silence they saw a rainbow arch above the Mountains of the Mist. For the very first time the butterflies looked all around. And as they looked, something wonderful happened!

Perhaps it was the enormous power released
by the lightning. Or was it the unusual hush after
the storm? Perhaps it was the butterflies' new awareness of
the beauty surrounding them. But as the bright sun warmed
them, their dull wings began to glow. Each butterfly was
touched with color! Some of their wings reflected the bright
flowers, the grasses and trees, the warm brown of the rocks
where each creature perched. Other wings took on the gold of
the sun, the blue of the sky, and the colors of the rainbow.

The butterflies stared at one another for a long time. Not one
made a sound. Finally, an orange-and-brown butterfly
murmured, "How astonishing—we're all different colors."

A large blue butterfly agreed softly, "Yes, our wings
have become as colorful as the earth around us, as bright
as the sun and sky."

Another whispered, "Just look at how beautiful all of you are!"

And the smallest butterfly, its voice a wisp of wind, added,
"You too!"

Awed by their transformation, not one butterfly thought to brag or argue. Not one of them wanted to shatter the quiet. Instead each butterfly flew off on silent wings to gather nectar.

Now, all the other creatures in the land were struck by the power of the storm too. They marveled when they saw the clouds of rainbow-colored butterflies. But, most of all, they were amazed at the silence, the peace and pleasure of it. For the rest of that day no monkey howled. No lion roared. And the herds of wildebeests stood still. Very still. The only sounds were the faint rustle of wind-fingered leaves and the *swash* and *brumble* of the rushing river.

OF COURSE, the country between the Mountains of the Mist and the Singular Sea was still noisy at times. Monkeys howled and hyenas laughed once in a while. Elephants trumpeted and lions roared. And the thundering hooves of the wildebeests continued to make the ground shake. But ever since that enormous storm, the country was quiet much of each day. Very quiet. Now all the animals, from anteaters to zebras, could detect the *splat* of raindrops on the banana leaves, the *thump* of fruit falling from a fig tree. And the elephants' ears flapped free.

From time to time, when two small figures strolled hand in hand through the land on the way to visit their old Juju, they no longer needed to run from the noise. Instead they would stop to smell the flowers and linger to admire all the brightly colored creatures. Butterflies would gently light on their arms and perch on their heads. Delighted, the boy would laugh and exclaim, "Pretty. So pretty."

Looking around, the girl often asked, "I wonder what happened to all those ugly, dull-winged insects—so noisy they made our ears throb?"

AS FOR BUTTERFLIES TODAY, perhaps they still speak, but as they drift from flower to flower or pause on the twig of a tree, each voice is so soft that only other butterflies can hear it. Everywhere the air is thick with brilliant color as the butterflies go by on silent wings.